JUST PLAIN BOB
HOT EROTIC EXPERIENCE

When
Rob *Met* *Kari*

WARNING

This book contains sexually explicit scenes and adult language. It may be considered offensive to some readers. This book is for sale to adults ONLY.

* * * * * * * * * * * * * * * * * * *

Please store your files wisely where they cannot be accessed by underage readers.

Please feel free to send me an email. Just know that these emails are filtered by my publisher. Good news is always welcome.

Just Plain Bob - **justplainbob@awesomeauthors.org**

About the Publisher
4Fun Publishing, a member of **BLVNP Incorporated**, 340 S. Lemon #6200, Walnut CA 91789, info@blvnp.com / legal@blvnp.com
NOTE: Due to the highly emotional reaction of some people to works of erotic fiction, any email sent to the above address that contains foul language or religious references is automatically deleted by our anti-spam software and will not be seen. All other communications are welcome.

DISCLAIMER
Please don't be stupid and kill yourself. This book is a work of FICTION. Do not try any new sexual practice that you find in this book. It is fiction and not to be confused with reality. Neither the author nor the publisher or its associates assume any responsibility for any loss, injury, death or legal consequences resulting from acting on the contents in this book. Every character in this book is over 18 years of age. The author's opinions are not to be construed as the opinions of the publisher. The material in this book is for entertainment purposes ONLY. Enjoy.

When Rob Met Kari
Hot Erotic Experience

By: Just Plain Bob

© Just Plain Bob 2014
ISBN: 978-1-68030-090-1

Part 1

It had been a long day. A 'brown out' had slowed things down at work and it couldn't have happened at a worst time. The production run was already behind and we were up against a hard deadline. The contract had penalties for failure to deliver on time and we would have to work overtime on the weekend if we were to have any chance at all of meeting the deadline.

I was looking forward to a cold beer on the living room couch as I caught the news on CNN. There was a Harley in the driveway just behind Audrey's Hondo Civic and I wondered who it might belong to. I walked into the living room and found Audrey sitting on the couch with some guy who looked just like the typical 'biker' that you see portrayed in the movies and on TV. A vest with all kinds of badges, pins and patches over a shirt with the sleeves torn off. Jeans, engineer boots completed the costume. His arms and hands were covered with tattoos and even without seeing them I would bet that he had a "hate" tattoo on his left hand and a "love" tattoo on his right.

Audrey stood up as I walked into the room and said, "Good. Now we can get this over with."

"Get what over with, Aud?"

"I'm leaving you Rob."

That came as a surprise to me as I'd not seen any indication of her dissatisfaction with me or our marriage. I looked at the guy sitting on the couch and smirking at me while holding a beer that I'd bet came from my stock in the fridge. I nodded toward him and said:

"With this piece of shit?"

He didn't like that and he started to get up. I ignored him and said to Audrey:

"Good luck with your new life."

I didn't waste any time with "Why?" or "What have I done?" or any of that other bullshit. If she was leaving and had asshole there to hold her hand it meant that she had already stabbed me in the back and cheated on me with him so she was history in my books. I turned to go to the kitchen and get me a beer and then the biker said:

"That's it? Your bitch tells you she is dumping your ass and all you say is have a nice life? Oh well, she said you would be a wimp."

I turned and looked at Audrey. "Did you say that? Did you tell asshole here that I was a wimp?"

Audrey looked away from me and I had my answer. I turned to the asshole and hit him. It caught him by surprise. Wimps aren't supposed to get violent, right? He shook it off and came after me. He must have been still thinking of me as a wimp because he didn't use any caution at all. He just rushed at me. I kicked the inside of his right knee and drove it outward and he screamed and went down as the knee gave way. I kicked him twice in the stones, lifted him up and slammed him against the wall and then I beat the living shit out of him. The entire time Audrey was screaming, "Stop it, stop it" but I ignored her. When I got tired I let him slump to the floor. I looked over at Audrey and said:

"How's that for being wimpy, Aud?"

I grabbed asshole by his feet and drug him outside and left him lying on the driveway next to his bike and then I went into the garage and got the half inch drive breaker bar and a screwdriver out of my tool box and went back to where the asshole was lying on the ground and moaning. I used the breaker bar to bust every light on the bike and then I carved "The wimp did this" into the paint on his gas tank.

I went back into the house and found Audrey sitting on the couch crying and I said:

"I hope you know how to ride his bike because I don't think he is in shape to do it."

"I can't drive a motorcycle. I'm taking my car."

"Oh no you aren't" I said as I grabbed her purse and dumped it out on the coffee table. I picked up her keys as I said "That car still has my name on the title and we still owe on it. I don't trust you to make the payments and I'll be damned if I'm going to let you ruin my credit."

Then I noticed the white envelope with First National Bank on it and I picked it up and looked inside. It was stuffed with money. I took my cell phone off my belt and hit the speed dial number for the bank. I punched in our account number and the mechanical voice said:

"Your checking account balance is six dollars and thirteen cents. Press two for withdrawal information. Press three for…"

I disconnected and snarled, "You bitch. You fucking whore! A house payment due, a car payment due and you cleaned me out and were going to leave me here holding the bag."

I picked up her wallet and took everything out of it except her driver's license and tossed it to her.

"Get out. Get your worthless ass out of here before I lose it and do to you what I did to that asshole you brought into my house."

"All my things are in the car."

"I'll clean the car out and dump your shit in the driveway. Anything still there on trash day will go out on the curb with the rest of the garbage now get the fuck out of here."

She walked out the door sniffling and sobbing and I went to the fridge to get another beer. As I pulled the tab on the can I had a thought so I set the beer down on the kitchen table and went back outside. Audrey was digging through the car for something and the biker was sitting up, leaning against his bike and retching. I walked up and looked down at him.

"I know your type asshole. I know just what you are going to do. You are going to round up some buddies and come back here to show me that I can't fuck with you and get away with it. I know you are going to do it and so I'll be watching out for you. I'm warning you now that if I see your ass again I'll do more than just beat the fuck out of you. Remember that asshole. You have been warned."

I went back into the house and about a half hour later I heard the Harley start up and drive off.

I was in the living room getting asshole's empty beer can off of the coffee table when I noticed a leather jacket lying on the floor next to the couch. I picked it up and on the back was painted a skull and the words "Diablo Riders." I looked at it for a few seconds and then I called my cousin Lou who was a sergeant on the local police force and asked him if he knew anything about the Diablo Riders.

"Only that they are a bunch of bad mother fuckers. They are into dope dealing and prostitution, but we haven't been able to hang anything on them. Why do you want to know about them?

I told him and he laughed. "I guess I know what Audrey will be doing this time next week. They'll have her hooked on something and she will be out on the streets making money for them. But you have a problem, cuz. They can't allow what you did to go un-avenged. It might give other people ideas."

***

I was watching the pregame show on Monday night football when the call came. I turned off the TV and went out and sat down on the front porch swing. Just a little over an hour later a car and two pickup trucks pulled up in front of the house and seven guys got out. One of them was asshole and I was pleased to see that he was walking with a cane. They came up the walk and I went down off the porch to meet them. One of them, a big ugly bearded dude said:

"You fucked up man. You don't mess with one of our guys and get away with it."

"I would suggest that you get off my property and do it now."

"Oh we will be going shit face, but not until after we teach you a lesson."

Two men moved in on me, one on each side and then the ugly dude swung at me. I didn't try to avoid the punch; I just stood there and took it. All hell broke loose as cops came spilling out of the house and garage and police cars with lights flashing and sirens going roared up the street and pulled up in front of the house. It all distracted the ugly dude and I speared him in the throat with the stiffened fingers of my right hand. At the same time I kicked the right knee of the guy on my right and he went down. The guy on my left was already running, but he didn't get far before two cops had him on the ground and were cuffing him.

Ugly dude lay at my feet gasping for breath and the other guy was clutching his knee and moaning. The rest of the group were all in handcuffs and being led away. All except asshole. He was standing there leaning on his cane as he watched his buds being loaded into the back of cop cars. My cousin Lou and another officer led him into the garage, sat him down on a chair and then cuffed him to it. Lou showed me two small cellophane bags and said:

"We found this on him. It is enough to take him down for possession with intent to sell. What do you want me to do?"

"Dump it or lose it. I don't want him in jail. I want him out where I can get to him."

Lou handed me the keys to the handcuffs and then he and the other officer left. I walked over to my tool box and brought out the half inch drive breaker bar and then walked back over to stand in front of asshole. I stood there lightly tapping my palm with the breaker bar and then said:

"They call this a breaker bar because it can usually break loose a stubborn nut or bolt. But you might remember that it can also break things. Remember the lights on your scooter? Remember what I told you the last time I saw you? I told you that if I ever saw you again I'd do more than just beat the fuck out of you, but you didn't listen did you. Did you see the punch that your buddy threw at me? Did you see me just stand there and take it? That was the price I had to pay to get you in this chair. I had to take that punch so it could be caught on tape to show just cause for the cops to take down your friends. Maybe they will thank you for giving them the opportunity to spend some time in jail. Think?"

I swung the breaker bar at his right knee as hard as I could and he screamed. I grabbed a shop towel from my work bench and forced it into his mouth to quiet him down and then I beat his right knee into mush. He had passed out from the pain so he was dead weight when I loaded him into the back of my pick up. I drove to a park just outside of town, pulled him out of the truck and dropped him by the pay phone just outside the public toilets. I checked his pockets to make sure that he had enough change to call for help and when I saw he didn't I put two quarters in his pocket.

I woke him up with some smelling salts and when I had his attention I told him:

"I warned you last time and you ignored it. You can ignore this warning too if you want to and it won't bother me at all. You like western movies? You know the part where one guy says to the other

"This town isn't big enough for both of us. You have until sundown to get out of town?" That's where we are now. Here's the deal. You need to leave this town and never come back. In two weeks I'm going to start looking for you and if I find you, depending on the mood I'm in, I'll either kill you or put you in a wheelchair for the rest of your life and you will be taking all of your meals through a straw. One last thing. What happened to you tonight didn't come from me. Call whoever you want and file any complaint you feel like, but I have five cops who will swear that I was playing cards with them. Remember. Two weeks and I come looking."

I left him there and drove home.

Lou called me in the morning. The biker's vehicles had dope and weapons galore in them. Three of the bikers had guns on them and two of the gun totters were on parole so they were on their way back to prison. Two were carrying knives longer than the law allowed and all of them had dope on them. They were all going to be going to jail for a while.

"The Tri-County Drug Task Force owes you and they told me to tell you that they have you covered."

"What does that mean?"

"What it means is that unless you do something totally stupid you will probably never again get a ticket in the Tri-County area in this life."

Two days later, he called me again. "I talked with Audrey last night. She is staying with her sister. I told her what she almost got herself into and she said that she already knew and that is why she is at her sisters. Seems that after the boys headed for your place to pay you a visit some of the girls in the clubhouse clued her in and she split and went to her sisters. She asked me to call you and ask you if she could come home and talk to you."

"No thanks, cuz. She said it all when she told me she was leaving me and when I found out she had cleaned out the bank account it was all over."

"Okay Rob, just passing a message. Be careful. There are still a couple of Diablo Riders still out there. They aren't really hardcore which is why they weren't with the bunch that came to visit, but better safe than sorry. Given your good standing with the Task Force we could probably get you a concealed carry permit if you want."

"Thanks Lou; I'll have to think on that."

***

Two weeks went by and one night when I came home from looking for asshole I found a woman sitting on my front porch steps. She stood up as I approached and I saw that she was a sexy looking woman although in a hard way if you know what I mean. I'm no judge of tit size, but hers were substantial and the tank top she was wearing showed plenty of cleavage. About five foot six, dishwater blond hair and she filled out her jeans nicely and altogether she looked like a lady I wouldn't mind playing with. The only thing I saw that I didn't care for were the tattoos she had. She had the 'barbed wire' one on her left arm and what looked like a bunch of flowers on her right arm at the shoulder. She probably had a couple more that I couldn't see. I walked up to her and asked:

"What can I do for you?"

"I just had to come by and get a look at the man who was bad enough to chase DJ out of town."

"And you are?"

"I was DJ's squeeze. I don't know if I should kiss you for making him leave or kick you in the balls."

"Why the big spread?"

"On the one hand I'm glad he's gone, but on the other it screws me up big time."

"How's that?"

"The rent is due and he split with the money. We've been late a couple of times before and the landlord said that the next time we were late we were out. Oh well, it won't be the first time we have had to sleep in the car."

She looked me up and down and the said, "Amazing. You don't look anything at all like a hard ass."

She started to walk away and I called out "Hey!" She turned back to me and I said:

"Don't leave me in suspense here. The kick or the kiss?"

She smiled, walked back to me, put her arms around me and kissed me. "Thanks" she said as she turned to go and I said "You said we when you mentioned sleeping in the car."

"I have two daughters."

"Your landlord will really kick you out if you are late with the rent?"

"He said he would and that's all I have to go on."

I was probably making a big mistake, but my thinking was that asshole was all set to leave with my woman so what better than him to find out that I was with his. Also, if he came back for her I wouldn't have to look as hard to find him.

"Can you cook?" I asked her before she could get away.

"Why?"

"I'm not that great in the kitchen and thanks to your ex-roomie I don't have a cook and housekeeper any more. It's a four bedroom house so there is plenty of room for you and your daughters. No strings attached. You will be the live in cook and maid and that's all."

"You serious?"

"You bet."

"Why would you do something like that?"

"He was all set to walk out of here with my wife. Imagine how he will take it when he hears that the woman that used to be his is now living with me. He won't know that all you are is a live in maid. He will think that we are doing the horizontal boogie and it will make him nuts. And I really can't cook for beans. As I see it it is a win win situation."

"Can I trust you?"

"Like I'm going to say no you can't? As long as your Honda keeps running you can leave whenever you think you can't trust me."

"When can I move in?"

"Right now if you want."

She gave me a long look and then said, "I'll need help moving my stuff and some of the guys who will help me are members of the Diablos. You sure you want them to know where you live?"

"They already know sweetie."

"Kari."

"Kari?"

"Kari is my name, not sweetie."

"Okay Kari" I said as I handed her the keys to my truck. "Give me the keys to the Honda. You can get the Diablos to help you load the truck, but we won't need them here. I'll take care of the unloading."

She looked at me with a strange expression and said, "The keys are in it. Why are you trusting me with your truck? That's a ten year old car parked at the curb and your truck is almost brand new."

"Trust has nothing to do with it Kari. If you aren't back in a reasonable amount of time I'll call it in as stolen and with all the friends I have on the local police force and in the county sheriff's office it won't take them any time at all to find it.'

I didn't mention the fact that the truck had Lo-Jack installed.

"Besides, I'm trusting that you want your daughters safe and not out on the streets if the landlord follows through on his threat."

She gave me another long look and then she turned and left.

She was back in three hours and as she got out of the truck I got my next surprise. I don't know why, but based on my best guess of Kari's age I imagined that her daughters would probably be around eight or nine so I was surprised when twin girls who looked every bit of twenty or twenty-one got out of the truck with her.

Kari walked up to me and as she handed me the keys to the truck she said, "Close your mouth before flies take up residence."

I looked at her. "No way. No way are you old enough to have twenty year old daughters."

"They are not twenty. They are an extremely well developed sixteen."

"Still, you are old enough to have daughters that age."

"Of course I am. I had them when I was fifteen."

She called the girls over and introduced them as Beverly and Barbara. They looked at me warily, but took my hand and shook it.

"Come on" I said, "Let me show you where you will be staying."

I led them into the house and took them on a tour which ended up on the second floor. I pointed out the three spare bedrooms and told them to take their pick. The three of the looked over the rooms, made their choices and then we went down and unloaded the truck.

Once they were moved in I told them that I hadn't been expecting company so the pantry was bare and I told Kari to check out the kitchen and the freezer in the basement and make a list of what we needed while I took a shower. I finished my shower, checked out Kari's list to see if there was anything I wanted to add and then we went shopping. I dropped Kari and the girls at King Soopers and told her I had an errand to run and would be back before they got to the checkout stands. I told her to buy enough to last us two weeks.

"Why two weeks?"

"Because I hate shopping."

I left them to shop and I drove over to Home Depot and picked up a few things and then drove back to the store. When we got home Kari said she would whip up something for dinner and I went out in the garage and rummaged through my tool box for what I would need.

We had a dinner of hamburger steaks and gravy with mashed potatoes and green beans and when everyone was done eating I reached down by my chair and pulled up the Home Depot bag. I took out the three packaged sets of keyed doorknobs and handed one to each of them.

"I know that all three of you are a little worried about what you might be getting into so I got you these. I'm giving them to you in the package so that you can see that it has not been opened so copies could be made of the keys and I want each of you to be standing there watching as I open the packages, give you the keys and install the doorknobs. I want all three of you to know that you are safe in this house."

I saw all three of them look at each other and maybe I just imagined it, but I thought I saw all three of them relax just a little.

"Okay then. A couple of rules to follow. Just as your rooms are off limits to me, mine is off limits to you. I have to get up at five to go to work so I'm usually in bed by ten or ten-thirty so try to keep the noise down after I sack out. There is a computer in the den and you are free to use it, but no porn sites. Porn sites are where most of the viruses come from. If there is anything in the kitchen that is especially yours label it otherwise what is in the fridge and pantry is up for grabs. And last of all I don't know if any of you smoke, but if you do the house is a smoke free zone. Outside on the patio or in the garage if the weather is bad, but never in the house. Those are mine. Do you have any?"

The two girls looked at each other and then one of them, I'm not sure which since I had not yet learned to tell them apart, asked:

"Can we have friends over?"

"Of course you can, but you are responsible for them while they are here."

"How about TV? Do you have any special shows we need to be aware of so we aren't on it when you want to be?"

"There are a couple but I have a set in my bedroom if need be. Oh, one other thing. I despise rap music so if you play it make sure that I don't hear it. Anything else?"

The three of them looked at each other and then Kari said, "I guess not, but if we think of something can we bring it up later?"

"Of course you can."

"Okay then" Kari said, "Come on girls, time to clear the table and clean the kitchen."

As they got up I asked myself again if I knew what I was doing and once again the answer was "hell no!"

I was sitting in front of the TV in the living room when the girls finished and Kari sent the twins off to do their homework and then she joined me on the couch.

"I need to know some things Rob."

"Shoot."

"Is this just something temporary, just a couple of weeks maybe, while you work on some plan concerning DJ?"

"Not at all. I admit that it concerns DJ, but the time limit on your stay is up to you. That of course is subject to change if I end up with another woman in my life, but I don't see that happening until I can legally get rid of the whore I'm married to and my information is that that little chore can take as long as six months. Why? Are you worried that I'm going to kick you out in a week or two?"

"I'm not very trusting when it comes to me Rob. They have taken advantage of me and fucked over me most of my life. It hasn't helped any that I've made bad choices. I need to know if it is worth the time and effort to get the girls transferred from the school they are in to the one in this district."

"That's strictly up to you. All I can say is that you can stay here until you decide that you don't want to or until I have a new lady in my life and she objects to our arrangement."

"Okay. You need to know that I have a job. I wait tables at Patty Ann's Café on the morning shift. I get off at two so I'll still have plenty of time to take care of my duties here as cook, maid and chief dishwasher. Between me and the girls we will get the job done."

"So you could have paid the rent at your old place?"

"Not hardly. I make enough to buy groceries and keep the girls in what they need. It is enough to take care of me if I was alone and living in a small one bedroom or studio apartment somewhere, but nowhere near enough to take care of the three of us in a place big enough for the three of us. DJ took care of the rent and utilities and I took care of the food and housekeeping."

"So what happened that I got a kiss for kicking him out of your life?"

"He kept trying to get me to do drugs with him. He said sex was so much better when on a drug high, but I wasn't buying it. I knew if he got me to try drugs I'd end up hooked and I'd already seen what other Diablos did to the women they got hooked. And then there were the girls. DJ's friends were starting to pay too much attention to them. I'll give DJ credit. He wouldn't stand for any one messing with Barb and Bev, but I began to get the idea that that was because he wanted them for himself. I was already looking for a way out when you did whatever it was that made him run. What did you do?"

I told her the story and she looked at me and said, "That's why I'm here isn't it? You expect him to come for me and that is what you are hoping for right?"

"It was a thought, but now that I've heard your story I don't think it is likely. I do hope that somehow he hears that you are living here with me. It should make him crazy."

"Not that I care any, but why take it out on him because your wife was going to leave you? If she could do it that easily shouldn't you have been thankful that he was getting her out of your life?"

"If he had kept his mouth shut and just left I wouldn't have bothered with him at all, but when he started that wimp shit I couldn't let it stand any more than I could turn my back on him coming after me with his buddies."

"Would you really cripple him for life if you see him again?"

"Absolutely. Threats and promises aren't worth spit unless you follow through on them. Too many people know about what I told the asshole and if the people don't see me follow through the word will get around that I don't mean what I say and I can't be having that."

"You told the girls they could have friends over as long as they take responsibility for them. Does that apply to me also?"

"Of course, but remember what I said; hold the noise down after I've gone to bed."

She blushed. "I don't have anybody waiting in the wings. It is too soon. DJ hasn't been gone long enough for me to start looking for a replacement, but it will happen sooner or later. I'm a healthy girl with healthy appetites. When it happens I'll try not to bring them here, but I did want to clear the decks just in case."

"Consider them cleared."

***

Surprisingly enough it worked. Kari and the twins took turns cooking and between the three of them they kept the house cleaner than it had ever been.

The Girls changed schools and they seemed to be good students. Kari worried about them a lot and she hovered over them like a momma bear over her cubs. She was afraid, and justifiably so, that a pair of sixteen year olds who looked twenty would be hit on a lot by the older boys and it scared her to death because that is what happened to her.

She had been an impressionable and extremely well developed fourteen when the eighteen year old seniors at her high school started hitting on her. She got all starry eyed and believed one of the assholes when he told her that he loved her and then she watched as he ran like a thief in the night when he got her pregnant. She kept telling the girls to be careful because she didn't want them to end up like her.

The arrangement was in its fourth week when a surprising development took place. Bev came up to me while I was on the computer in my den and her mother and sister were in the kitchen doing the dinner dishes.

"Can I ask you something?"

"Sure, go ahead."

"Are you gay?"

"Hell no. Why would you think something like that?"

"Why haven't you made a move on my mom? She is as horny as a billy goat and is ready for a man. Does she need to carry a sign saying "*F*uck me please" before you pay attention to her?"

"Maybe it is because your mom hasn't shown any interest in having a move made on her. Maybe it is because I'm still married and I don't feel right about going after other women before I'm divorced. Maybe it is because I have the hots for someone else."

And then, probably because I was a little pissed at her thinking I was gay and a little upset with her attitude, I decided to shock her and I said:

"And just maybe it is because I want you and Barb and not your mother."

"I expected her to turn purple and run from the room, but she looked me right in the eye and said:

"As long as you understand that it won't be without a condom."

I'm not sure, but I think I'm the one who turned purple. Bev gave me a little smile and turned and left the room. As I watched her walk I realized that Kari I had good reason to be scared. And so did I. I was painfully aware of the hard on that Bev has just given me.

***

From then on the tone of things changed around the house. Bev and Barb (apparently they kept no secrets from each other) started openly flirting with me when Kari wasn't around. I became aware that it was being offered to me if I was ready and willing to step up to the plate.

And no, it was not just my imagination.

Kari left the house at four-thirty to open Patty Ann's Café and get things set up for the breakfast crowd. I was up and ready to leave the house between five and five-fifteen and until the night that Bev came into the den the twins were never up until after I was gone. Suddenly, once Kari was gone, the twins were getting up and trotting between their bedrooms and the bathroom naked! It was obvious that I was being deliberately tempted. And tempted I was. God knows I was. But I was also smart enough to know that slipping my cock into a sixteen year old, no matter how desirable she might be, was a one way ticket to a dark and gloomy jail cell.

About a week after the girls started running around naked in front of me I took a day off from work to go to the doctor's and get my yearly physical so I was still in the house at seven-thirty. The girls normally left the house for school around ten to eight. I was sitting at the computer checking my email when the girls came into the room. Barb said:

"We want to know which of us you want to do first."

"I'm not going to do either one of you."

"Sure you are. Sooner or later one of us will get you so why fight it?"

"There are all kinds of reasons for me to fight it. You are under age and when I got caught I would go to jail and I would get caught because your mom watches you too close. That's one and another is that your mom would kill me if she even thought I may have the idea of doing either of you. Then there is the health issue. No way I would be physically able to handle the both of you so forget it girls; it just ain't gonna happen."

"We don't hear you saying you don't want to, just that you are afraid to."

"And that is reason enough right there."

Bev said, "First off the only reason mom is worried is because she doesn't want us to end up as single moms at our age. That won't ever happen because even though mom doesn't know it we are both on the pill thanks to an older friend of hers who pretended to be our mom when we went to the doctor and if you'll remember I already told you that you would have to use a condom. You won't go to jail because no one but the three of us will ever know. Your health won't be an issue because we will set up a schedule and take turns. You can come up with all the excuses you want, but we have made up our minds so it is going to happen."

She looked at her watch and said, "Got to run or we will miss the bus. While you are out today load up on condoms" and then she and Barb left.

***

As I sat in the waiting room at the doctor's office I was wondering how you were supposed to handle a pair of sixteen year olds that looked twenty and acted twenty-five. The best that I could come up with is that I was going to have to sit down with Kari and clue her in to what was going on.

Was I scared? To death man, to death.

I made sure not to go home before I knew Kari would be there. I did not want to be alone with Bev and Barb. I knew what I wasn't going to do, but I didn't know what they might do so I thought it best to avoid them.

Dinner was almost ready when I did get home and I went into the bathroom to wash my hands and in the mirror over the sink I saw Barb come in behind me. She opened her blouse to show me that she didn't have a bra on and she cupped her tits in her hands and pointed them at me and said:

"Still want to say no?"

I ignored her and she laughed and left the room. Barb was sitting opposite me at the dinner table and even though I'm not a lip reader I had no trouble making out the word when she looked at me and silently mouthed the word "chicken." It made me even more determined to have a talk with Kari and I decided to do it when she sent the girls off to do their homework. During the time between dinner ending and the girls being sent off to their rooms I rehearsed what I would say to Kari, but then I started thinking 'what if she doesn't believe me? What if she goes to the girls and they say that it is all bullshit and that I've been hitting on them and now I'm trying to make trouble for them because they kept saying no. What if…..? By the time they were sent off to do their homework I did what Barb had silently accused me of. I chickened out.

The next morning I made sure that I was up and out of the house a minute behind Kari. I would handle the problem with the girls by making sure that I was never alone with them. The Waffle House was open all night so I had a place to go to have breakfast and nurse a cup of coffee until it was time to go to work. That got old after two days so I knew I would have to find some other early morning activity to get me out of the house. I was looking through the morning paper and saw an ad announcing the grand opening of a fitness center and it said that the hours of operation would be from five in the morning until nine at night. It was $395 a year and I considered that a fair price if it kept me away from Bev and Barb.

I would be up and out of the house at the same time as Kari. I had to wait at the door of the fitness center until it opened at five. At the end of the day, I made sure that I never went home until I knew Kari would already be there. That became my new schedule.

***

While all that drama was taking place at home, there was even more drama away from home. Both had their origins in my confrontation with Audrey and DJ.

Kari has kept in touch with one or two of her girlfriends lucky enough not to be in jail and who were still running with the Diablos. They told her that the word was that as soon as the ones I had caused to be locked up got out they would be coming for me. I called Lou and told him that I was interested in the concealed carry permit he had mentioned.

. I already had a Beretta 92F. He put me in touch with the people I had to talk with. After a twelve-hour course, I had a permit to carry.

I tried to visit a couple of Diablos who were in prison, but found out that the only way you could get on the approved visitor's list was if the inmate requested that you to be on it. I finally got one, who was curious enough about why I wanted to visit, to put me on his list. I went to see him on a Saturday. He sat on the other side of the glass partition. I could tell from the smirkish smile on his face that he knew what was planned for me so I cut right to the chase.

"The reason I wanted to see you was to give you the chance to save your life."

The smirk disappeared and was replaced by a what-the-fuck-you-talking-about look.

"Here's the deal. I've heard about what you say you are going to do to me when you get out; here is what I am going to do about it." I took my carry permit out of my shirt pocket and held it up to the partition so he could read it.

"They wouldn't let me bring the Beretta in here, but I don't go anywhere else without it. The way it is going to be is that if I see any one of you once you get out, I will kill you. If we run into each other in Safeway, I will take out my gun and kill you. If I am in a gas station putting gas in my car and I see you pulling in to get gas for your bike, I will kill you. If I'm driving down the street and I see you coming up from behind in the next lane, I will roll my window down and kill you when you get close enough. Get the message? If I see you anywhere at all, I'm going to remember that you said you were going to get me when you got out; I will kill you before you get the chance.

"All my friends in the sheriff's office and in the local police force know about your threat. They have already approved of what I have to do and they will make sure that it goes down as a justifiable homicide. So get your head around it. I will kill you if I see you. Tell all your buddies. If I see any of you, you will die. I will not wait for you to make a move and then defend myself. If I see you, then I will kill you. Have a nice day."

I got up and walked out of the visiting room. It was bullshit about the cops giving me a pass, but he didn't know that. He saw all the cops I had waiting when he and his crew showed up at my place. He also knew that DJ had been left in my hands when the rest of them were hauled away so I bet he believed me.

The other thing going on was that Audrey was fighting the divorce. All of a sudden I was the love of her life. She couldn't live without me, and everything that had happened was all just a huge misunderstanding. We could put things back together if I would just sit down with her and talk things out.

"Not a chance in hell," I told her through my attorney. She countered by having her attorney petition the court to order counseling, and so the judge ordered for it. It was one of those open-ended things that would go on and on until the counselor decided that there was no hope of reconciliation. Since he was paid for per session and not at a flat fee, he could drag it out forever.

The first session was about what were the major problems between us. I told him up front during the very first session that there was not the slightest chance that I would ever take the bitch back. I told him my side but Audrey kept butting in and telling me that I was wrong. That I just didn't understand the situation, and if I would only let her explain! I stood up and started to leave. The counselor asked me where I was going. I told him there was no sense in my staying there and trying to tell my side if he wasn't going to tell her to shut the fuck up and stop interrupting me. He told Audrey to keep quiet and that she would get her turn when I was finished. I sat down and finished my say with:

"Counseling is not going to do any good in this case. It will only work if both parties want to see if they can save the marriage. It won't work here because there is no way I am staying with a lying, cheating, and thieving whore."

Then it was her turn. She said she had never cheated on me and she wasn't really leaving me. It was just going to be a trial separation to give her some time and space to work on some issues she had with our marriage. She wasn't running off with DJ. He was just a friend she had with her in case I tried to stop her from leaving. And, she didn't mean to take all of the money out of our account. She only meant to take half but she was nervous, sweating coming from the confrontation with me. That her mind was elsewhere when the bank teller told her our balance so she automatically wrote it on the withdrawal slip. She realized the mistake on her way home and she intended to give me half the money before she left, but I never gave her the chance. The bottom line was that she loved me, really, really loved me, it was all just a huge mistake, and that we could work things out.

The counselor said that was enough for that session. He told us to make a list of the issues we individually saw in the marriage and bring it during the next session to discuss. I wanted to tell him that there wouldn't be any more sessions but I couldn't. My lawyer already told me that the divorce was stalled until the court had the report from the marriage counselor saying that no hope of a reconciliation existed. No counselor was going to say that without at least four sessions.

The second session was more bullshit from Audrey, as she listed the issues she had while I listened and shook my head. I dropped my dirty clothes on the floor. I left the toilet seat up. I never called when I was going to be a little late in coming home. I got up Saturday morning and cut the grass even though I knew she liked to sleep in on weekends, and the mower motor would wake her up. She was willing to watch football with me, but I would never watch Oprah with her and so on and on and on. She made herself look like an absolute doofus.

He asked for my list and I told him that I didn't have one. I told him I was perfectly happy with my marriage right up to the day when she and DJ ambushed me in our living room. Actually, I didn't say it quite that way. What I said was: "Until the whore cheated on me and tried to steal my money."

"I explained all of that, honey."

"And I don't believe a word of it."

Then the counselor said that the next session would be a one-on-one with Audrey followed by a one-on-one with me. After which, he would decide whether or not we needed to go any further. After Audrey had gone, I asked him what good it would do to have the one-on-ones when he already knew that I wouldn't get back together with Audrey even at gunpoint.

"I have to do it because the judge ordered it. If it were Judge Harriman or Judge Spiegel, I could go back after one session and tell them there was no hope and say that further sessions would be a waste of time. Your judge and three or four others insisted on a minimum of four sessions. Be thankful your judge isn't Whitman. He has been known to specify eight or ten sessions. Before you ask, no, I won't let you not show up and say that you did. If your wife or her attorney found out somehow, I would be toast. The best I can do for you is to schedule your one-on-one on a Monday night, and we can watch Monday Night Football in the TV in my office."

And that is just what we did.

On my way home from watching the game, it suddenly occurred to me that I was being stupid. Audrey didn't want a divorce so by God I wouldn't give her one. We were in a no-fault state so she would end up with half of our assets. She couldn't touch the house because it had been left to me by my parents and I never added her name to the title or the mortgage. However, she would get half of the cash and household furnishings, one of the vehicles, a part of my pension, 401k when I retired, and probably some alimony because I made more than she did with her part-time morning job. No divorce, no divorce settlement.

Audrey was thinking no divorce meant she would move back in, but that would be a cold day in hell.

I called Audrey as soon as I got home and told her that after having my session with Henry, the counselor, I decided to drop the divorce.

"When can I come home?"

"When hell freezes over. I'm dropping the divorce because I'm not going to waste any more of my time fighting with you over it, but I still don't want anything to do with your lying, cheating ass," and I hung up on her.

I knew it wouldn't be the end, but it would take her a while to figure out what to do next and more importantly come up with money to do anything about it. The next morning, I called my attorney and told him to do what needed to be done to stop the divorce proceedings.

Back at home, I was still doing everything I could to avoid being alone with Barb and Bev. They were tempting as hell, and I had been without long enough that I occasionally had some impure thoughts where they were concerned. Thank God, my big head was still in charge.

Part 2

The one thing I never expected happened. I woke up in the middle of the night with my dick being sucked. My first thought was that Bev or Barb had snuck into my room and were just going to take what I would not give on my own. I tensed and was gathering myself to rise and push whichever twin it was off of me when a voice said:

"Relax, baby, we both need this."

The voice was Kari's. She swung over me, took my cock in her hand, lined it up, and pushed down on it. It had been a while for me and I did not last as long as I would have liked to, but it didn't bother Kari.

"It has been a while for me too, baby, but don't worry because we aren't done yet."

She went back to work on my cock and I responded to her ministrations. The second time was a lot longer and more satisfying. When it was over Kari said, "I want to stay and cuddle. I want my girls to see me leave your room in the morning."

I opened my arms and she snuggled in.

I woke up when she got out of bed. "It's early," she said, "you have another hour or so until your alarm goes off. I just heard one of the girls go into the bathroom so I'm going to leave your room as she comes out into the hallway. I want her to see me."

She bent over, kissed me, and said, "Until tonight, baby." She moved over to the door, hesitated until she heard the bathroom door open, and then she stepped out of my room into the hall.

***

At work, I got a call from Kari asking me to meet her at Miller's Bar when I got off. When I got there, she was sitting in a table where two guys stood there, talking to her. She saw me and waved over me. When I got there, she stood, kissed me, and then sat down.

"Guys, this is my boyfriend, Rob. Rob, this is Stan and Jerry."

The guys shook my hand and said, "Nice meeting you"; then told Kari that they would see her around, and walked away.

She smiled and said, "That worked out well."

"What worked out well?"

"Killing two birds with one stone: First, I needed to talk with you away from the house. Second, those two will spread the word about my boyfriend. That will shut down some of the assholes who keep bothering me."

"I'm your new boyfriend?"

"You are if you want to be."

"What do you need to talk about away from the house?"

"Last night. I need to explain it."

"Why?"

"Because I don't know if you are okay with it. If you aren't, I need to explain why so you don't throw us out on our butts."

"Did I behave like I was unhappy about it?"

"No, but how you feel when Mr. Happy is busy is not an indication of how things are when he is resting."

"So what is to explain?"

"I was super horny and I needed to get laid. I've been trying to find someone who would turn me on since I've moved in with you, but I haven't had much luck. There were a lot of horn dogs like Stan and Jerry, but none I could really get interested in except you. However, I stayed away from you because you didn't seem all that interested in me other than something that could piss off DJ."

"What changed your mind?"

"Barb and Bev."

"How did they change your mind?"

"I was in the laundry room folding clothes, and they thought that I was up in my room so they were talking unaware that I could hear them. I heard all about their plans to get you to do them. I knew that the only way I could stop it was to get to you first and then let them find out about it so they would leave you alone."

"You didn't have to worry. They have been wagging their butts at me for two weeks now, and I have avoided them. Believe me, I wouldn't have touched them."

"Oh yes, you would have. What I did last night was what they had planned on doing. They were going to flip a coin to see which one of them was going to sneak in and wake you with a blow job. If one of them had gotten you up and hard, there is no doubt in my mind that you would have not stopped."

"I've been expecting them to pull something and I have a great sense of self-preservation. My fear of going to jail over having sex with a minor had put me to a stop as soon as I realized what was going on. You saw it yourself. You felt me getting ready to push you away and that is why you told me to relax. It is only because I recognized your voice that you didn't end up on your butt on the floor."

"But you didn't push me away and I'm glad. I enjoyed myself and I'd like to do it again. In fact I'd like to do it on a steady basis. How do you feel about that?"

"As I recall, you kissed me and said, 'Until tonight,' when you left my room.

I could not believe when I said, "No way! Not gonna do it."

She smiled at me and said, "It has been a while for me. Early tonight?"

***

Outside of the nasty looks the twins gave me and a bi-weekly phone call from Audrey saying that she knew we could work things out if I would just talk to her, the next three months passed by uneventfully. Work was going well, Kari and I were having sex three or four times a week, and the twins were doing well in school and had gotten involved in girls volleyball and field hockey.

Then Audrey reared up and threw shit into the game.

She had saved up enough money to get an attorney and she had filed for a legal separation. The judge —a different one—ordered counseling so we started all over again. We had a different marriage counselor so everything was new to him.

Audrey was acting differently during the first mandated session. I told my side the same as I had done previously, and Audrey didn't try to interrupt me. When it was her turn, she calmly said, "I filed for a separation rather than a divorce because I don't want a divorce. My attorney also said that a separation would be the best way to get a court order for counseling. I believe that if I can just sit down with Rob and explain things we can work things out.

"First, I need to clear up a couple of things: Rob accused me of being a cheating whore and that is not true. I have never cheated on him and I'm perfectly willing to take a lie detector test for that. DJ was there with me that day to help me if you got violent. Before you explode on me for saying that, I will admit that never in our marriage did you ever raise a hand on me. But then I had never told you that I was walking out on you either. I had no way of knowing how you would react and that is why DJ was there. The other thing is that I was called a thief and I deny that. The way I explained it in previous sessions is just the way it happened. I would have given half of it back, but I never got the chance. I'll take a lie detector test for that also.

"I made some errors in judgment. I should have handled things differently and I know that now. I should have sat down with you, explained why I wanted a trial separation, and then discussed it. But as we all know, hindsight is twenty-twenty."

Then Barry, the counselor, said, "Now that you have brought it up, I suppose you can tell us why you wanted that trial separation."

"I wanted some excitement in my life. Marriage with Rob was dull and boring. We never went anywhere or did anything. I love Rob and our sex life was good, but I wanted a little more than that. I talked with my girlfriend Anna two or three times a week, and she was always telling me about the fun things she was doing. After a while, I started wanting to do some fun things too. One of the things I've always wanted to do was try pot, but Rob has always been a rabid anti-drug person. I wanted to drink and dance all night long. Although Rob drinks, he doesn't dance so he never took me anywhere I could dance with someone else if they asked me. Of course, knowing Rob, I know he would never let me dance with anyone else even if he took me to a place where it could happen.

"One afternoon Anna talked me into going out and spending an afternoon with her. We went to a bar on the other side of town and she introduced me to some of her friends. We drank and danced to the music on the juke box, and a couple of guys asked us if we wanted to go for a ride. It was my first time on a motorcycle and I loved it. I started spending one or two afternoons a week with Anna and her friends.

"One day DJ was there and he asked me if I'd like to take a ride with him. I said yes. We rode for almost an hour. Then he pulled in, parked in a picnic area, and asked me if I would like to share a joint with him. It was something I had always wanted to try so I said yes. I liked it. I liked the feeling that it gave me. When the joint was gone, we rode back to the bar. After that, DJ always seemed to be there whenever I went out with Anna. He always asked me if I wanted to go for a ride.

"Most of the time there were half-dozen bikers on the run, and we always ended up somewhere where we did a little smoke. I always made sure I was home on time to have the dinner ready for Rob when he got home from work. One day DJ made a pass at me, and I shut him down. I told him I was married and I loved my husband. He didn't push it, just shrugged, but he was always the one offering the rides. He was always the one sharing his pot with me.

"I was having a ball, but I wanted more. I got the dumb idea of telling Rob I was going to leave him for a while to try and find myself. I discussed it with Anna and she suggested that I have someone with me to keep Rob from going off on me. I asked DJ if he would do it, and he said that he would. Then he asked me if I really expected trouble from Rob. I made the mistake of saying probably not, that Rob was usually a pussycat. So he said that what I was telling him is that Rob was a wimp. To my everlasting shame, I didn't say no to that. I just shrugged my shoulders and said that Rob probably was. The only reason I did that was so DJ wouldn't change his mind about going with me. If he thought Rob would be no trouble, he wouldn't back out.

"Anyway, it all went to hell when Rob came home and I told him I was leaving. He surprised me by just saying, 'Have a nice life,' and that is when DJ went all stupid on us; and here we are."

She turned to me and said, "I love you Rob and I don't want a divorce."

I just shrugged and said, "Okay, Audrey, I've listened to what you have said. Some or perhaps all of it may be true, but it changes nothing as far as I'm concerned. The day you told me you were leaving me for whatever reason is the day our marriage died. I wrote you off then and I see no reason to change my mind. By your own words here, I wasn't good enough for you then. I wasn't exciting enough for you then. Well I have news for you, Audrey: I'm still the same unexciting guy I was then and I'm never going to change. Taking you back would be the dumbest thing I could do. I could never trust that someday you wouldn't go off again to find your so-called excitement."

"You say that you never cheated on me with DJ or any of the others you had your excitement with. It could possibly be true, but I will never believe it. Assholes like DJ and the guys he ran with don't waste time on broads that don't put out. So there it is. You can force counseling all you want and you can fight any divorce I pursue, but you and I are done. There is no—I repeat, no—chance that you and I will ever get back together."

Barry looked from me to Audrey and then said, "Counseling only works when both parties want to work on saving the marriage. I can see that isn't the case here. I will file my report with the court, stating that I see no chance of reconciliation in this case.

Audrey cried out, "Damn it, Rob. I love you. You have to give me a chance."

"I gave you six years, Audrey, and it wasn't enough."

I got up, shook Barry's hand, thanked him for his time, and then walked out of his office. As I headed home, I made up my mind that I was not going to restart the divorce. Why waste money just so I could give my money and other assets to Audrey? Any divorce should be because she went for it.

***

The next six months went by quickly. Kari had moved into my bedroom much to the dismay of Bev and Barb, who seemed to still have desires over me. By then, I was treating them like daughters.

They had both taken Driver's Ed in school and had their temporary permits. They got As and Bs in their report cards and they were heavily involved in girl-sports. They were great kids except for their obsession with trying to get on my bed.

I spent a lot of time with them out on the road. When we were away from Kari, they flirted shamelessly with me, but I still wasn't having any of it. Finally I sat down with both of them and told them flat out that they were wasting their time.

"You are both underage, and I will not risk going to jail so give it a rest."

"So what I'm hearing," Bev said, "is that if we were eighteen it would be a done deal?"

I threw my hands up in exasperation and walked away from them.

***

A week before their seventeenth birthday, I sat down at the dinner table with them and told them that their mother and I had worked out a deal. I was going to give to their mother my ex's car, which was only two years old, in exchange for her ten-year-old car. They hood took their driver's test, passed, and got their permanent licenses. I was going to give them their mother's car as a birthday present. There were squeals of delight. They jumped, ran around the table, and then kissed and hugged me.

That night while Kari and I relaxed in each other's arms after making love, she said:

"Thank you, lover."

"For what?"

"For being the man you are. You are the closest thing to a father that the girls have ever had."

"You're kidding me?"

"No, I'm not. The men I've hooked up with have tolerated them, but only because they wanted me. There were some—like DJ—who tried to hide it from me, but saw them as fresh meat. I know that doesn't say much for me, but you can't always tell what kind a man is when you first start out with him. I wish I'd met you fifteen years ago."

"No, you don't. Fifteen years ago, I was a horny dog running around, trying to stick my dick into anything female."

"What changed you?"

"I grew up."

"Oh well, better late than never," she said as she fondled my cock.

***

It seemed that my life was destined to be full of surprises. The twins had several friends over on their birthday. We had a cake and ice cream. I handed a twenty to each of them. I handed to Bev—for she was the older, by three minutes—the keys to Kari's old car and told them to make sure that they were home by eleven.

After they and their friends were gone, Kari and I curled up on the couch and she said, "I talked with your wife today."

"You what?"

"I was in Safeway, picking up the cake and ice cream when she walked up to me and said 'hi.' I didn't know Audrey was your wife."

"Sure you did. There isn't a week that goes by that she doesn't get mentioned."

"Yes, but never by name. It was always 'that bitch I was married to' or 'my whore of an ex.' You never mentioned her by name."

"Why does it matter?"

"It doesn't, I guess. It's just that I knew her when she was hanging around with the Diablos with her friend Anna."

"Then you know what a whore she was."

"Actually I don't. The whole time she was around us, all she did was some drinking, dancing, and pot smoking. She liked going on rides, but she never did anything else. She might have wanted to, but she never did."

"So what did she want?"

"She heard that I was staying with you and wanted to know why I was trying to steal her man."

"Her man? That's a laugh."

"She thinks she can get you back if only I will get out of the way."

"Not a chance in hell with that."

"I told her I was not in her way—that I was just a boarder and that I got a room for being the maid and cook. I told her that the only reason you let me move in was so you could rub DJ's nose in it."

"And she bought that? That doesn't sound like Audrey."

"I told her I tried to get you in bed; but you pushed me away, said it wouldn't be right, and that you couldn't do anything like that until you were divorced. She really does plan on trying to get you back."

"You should have told her we were bed buddies, and maybe then she would have gotten the message that I'm done with her."

"I might have if it was anyone else; but I know she never cheated on you, at least not with our group, so I didn't think it would be fair. I liked her. I think she got stupid for a little bit and now she's trying to get back what she knows she should have never given up."

When I heard that, all I could do was shrug.

***

I started getting weekly phone calls from Audrey. The first one set the tone for all that followed.

"Kari tells me that you don't make love because you aren't divorced yet. I'm never giving you a divorce; so the question is: how long can you go without sex? Knowing you, I'm surprised that it has been this long. You don't have to go without it baby. I'm here for you any time. Just call me."

"Why don't you just go away, Audrey?"

"I can't, baby, I love you. I know I fucked up and I'm sorry, but I do love you and I'm going to get you back. It may take some time, but I'm going to get you back."

What the hell was with that woman, I thought as I hung up the phone. She couldn't wait to bail out on me and now she's all hot to come back. Why? She was out there. She was free to do whatever she wanted. She was a good looking and sexy looking, and I knew she would have plenty of guys sniffing around. So there she was: man bait; free to smoke pot, drink, and dance; and have all that excitement she wanted to experience that's why she was leaving me.. So, why the fuck was she bugging me to take her back? To me, it made no sense at all.

At home, even though Kari has staked her claim, the twins still took shots at me whenever she wasn't around. They thought nothing than walking naked in front of me. They would also come into the bathroom and try to catch me with my dick out in my hand while I was taking a whiz. Bev once came in and asked me if she could hold it and aim it for me. They did it even though I had a lock on the door—the knob was one you could open from the outside with a dime or even a long fingernail. I finally had to replace it with a keyed lock.

***

That was my life for the next six months. I work, make love to Kari three or four times a week, cut grass, do household chores, get a phone call from Audrey every two weeks or so, and fight off the attention of the twins.

They almost got me once and it was a close call. Kari had gone somewhere to do something. I was sitting on the easy chair ,watching something on the TV when I nodded off. Suddenly, I felt something on my chest. I woke up and saw Barb wrapping clothesline around me and the chair. Bev was doing the same thing to my legs and the chair legs.

When they were done, they stepped back to admire their handiwork and then Bev said, "Who gets him first?" They did rock-paper-scissors, and Barb won. She was just pulling down my zipper when they heard the garage door start to open.

"Shit! Mom's home."

They hurriedly unwrapped off of me and then ran to their rooms before Kari got into the house. I had thought that with me and Kari being involved, I would be okay; apparently, I wasn't. I resolved never to let myself be alone with them again.

Audrey's phone calls were sounding a little more desperate. "Please, baby, you have to let me come home. I don't know how much longer I can hold out."

"What do you mean 'hold out'?"

"I'm a healthy girl, Rob, and I haven't had sex since the last time with you."

"So go get yourself laid."

"I can't, baby. If I do, I know for sure that you will never take me back."

"Why didn't you think of that way back when you decided to bail out on me?"

"I wasn't thinking, Rob. I was just thinking of the fun I could have. I didn't wake up until I found out what DJ had planned for me. I'm sorry, Rob. I messed up big time but I will make it up to you. Please, baby, please let me come home."

"Why, Audrey? Just so I can spend my time wondering when you would get bored with me and go partying with Anna again?"

"I don't even talk to Anna anymore. She knew what was likely going to happen to me but she never warned me. She was a fucking Judas goat."

"I'm sorry, Audrey, but I just can't see it happening. Bye."

***

Kari got a call from one of her friends who told her that two of the Diablos in jail, having a year each, were out on early release so I started carrying my Beretta. About three weeks after getting the call, Kari and I were at the mall and I saw one of them. He saw me at the same time and he saw me open my coat and reach for the Beretta in the shoulder holster. He turned and ran into the other direction. I guess he got the message I had passed that day in the visiting room of the prison.

It was a week after that a disaster struck.

***

It was a Monday night and I was in the bathroom upstairs, changing a burned out light bulb, when I saw three guys come over the back fence. As they moved to the house, I noticed that one of them had a bad limp. I hurried to my bedroom, got the Beretta, and moved downstairs quietly. The stairs ended on a landing that led into the living room on the right and the dining room on the left. Kari and the twins were on the couch where they had been watching TV. The three men faced them and had apparently not heard me coming down.

As I reached the bottom, I heard DJ saying, "…three of you, whores, making money for me, but first I'm going to settle up with the fuck-face who lives here. Where is he?"

"Right behind you, sperm breath."

He spun around and I saw a gun in his hand. I already had mine up and I put three rounds on the center of his chest. As the others drove him backwards, he threw his arms out wide, and his gun went off. The two men put their arms up and cried, "Don't shoot, don't shoot."

I heard Bev and Barb scream. It took a second or two to register that they were screaming, "Mommy, mommy." I took a quick look and saw Kari slumped on the couch, blood running down on her front. "Call 911," I hollered, but both girls were hysterical. I kept the gun on the two men, hurried over, and slapped Bev. When she shook it off, I told her to call 911.

I walked over to DJ and kicked his gun away. He looked up at me and gasped, "I'm hurt bad. Call an ambulance, man. For God's sake, get me some help."

I leaned down and whispered in his ear, "I told you if I ever saw you again, I'd kill you. No ambulance for you, cocksucker. Lie there and die."

I told the two guys to lie down on their backs on the floor and spread their arms and legs like they were making angels in the snow.

"If you move, I will kill you. Raise your head, twitch, or do any movement at all and I will shoot you dead. I swear to God I will. I'm sorely tempted to do it anyway."

"Don't man, please don't. We were only supposed to help him get his bitches back. There wasn't supposed to be no shootin'. We want no part of this shit, man."

While holding the gun on them, I got Kari on her back and ripped open her blouse. I grabbed a throw pillow, put it over the bullet hole in her chest, and pushed down to try stop the bleeding. Her eyes fluttered open. She managed to lift her arm grab my wrist.

"My girls," she said weakly, "take care of my girls. Promise me, Rob, take care of my babies."

"I promise."

Her grip weakened, and then with a little cry she was gone. Bev and Barb were crying. Barb looked at me and asked, "Momma?"

All I could do was shake my head "no," and that set off more wailing.

After all of the flashing red and blue lights were gone and the girls and I were alone, I tried to calm them down But how do you do that to two girls who have just seen their mother get shot and then die in front of them? All I could do was put my arms around them and hug them as they cried in my shoulders. After a while, I led them to my bedroom. The three of us got on the king size bed—Barb on my right and Bev on my left. With an arm around each of them, I held them while they cried themselves to sleep.

***

On the next three days, we were busy with interviews from the detectives and assistant district attorneys and making arrangements for Kari's funeral. There were only a dozen or so who attended her funeral. One of them, a hard-looking redhead, came up to me and introduced herself as Matty. She shook my hand and told me that she was sorry for my loss.

"You were good for her. She was really happy for the first time in the eight years that I have known her. She was hoping to marry you if you ever divorced Audrey. It was the first time I ever heard her talk about marriage."

"You know Audrey?"

"She ran with us for a while until we clued her in on what DJ had planned for her."

"Why did you clue her in?"

"It was obvious to the rest of us that she didn't belong there. She was getting a taste of wild for the first time in her life, and it was turning her head. She wouldn't have lasted a week on the street. We knew it so we told her what she was getting herself into just in time for her to get out."

"I heard she was pulling trains with the guys in your club."

"I don't know who told you that shit, but she never gave it up for any of the guys even though nearly all of them tried. Not even DJ although he did brag about what he was going to do with her when he got her break in. Anyway, I kept Kari up-to-date on what the Diablos were planning, and if you want to give me your number, I'll call you if anything about you comes up." I gave her my number and she left.

It was a sad day for the twins, and they were not yet cried out so I had my hands full with trying to comfort them. Since that first night, we had all been sleeping on my bed and I was going to put an end to that soon. I didn't expect anything to happen until we got away from their mother's death; but given their track record in the past, it was likely that, one day in the future, I was going to be a target again.

During breakfast the day after Kari's funeral, both girls were sitting in the table with their eyes downcast. I assumed they were grieving so I didn't say anything. About halfway through breakfast, Bev set her fork down and said, "When do we have to leave?"

"Leave? Why are you leaving?"

"Mom's gone. None of her other boyfriends wanted us around even when she was there; and now she's gone."

"Yes she is, but I'm not. The last thing your mom said to me was, 'promise me that you will take care of my girls,' and I promised her that I would. You are my girls now and you aren't leaving unless you want to."

"You mean it?" Barb cried, "We can stay?"

"As long as you want."

They both jumped up and came over and hugged me. There was more crying, only that time it wasn't caused by sadness.

For the next two nights, they slept with me. One morning, I woke up with Barb's leg thrown over mine and her left hand on my thigh, about three inches away from home plate. I started getting stiff and I knew it was time to send them back to their own rooms. It was also time to step back and look at what I had promised Kari and where it was going to lead. There were no two ways about it. I was going to need protection from the twins and to be brutally honest with myself, they were getting very close to needing protection from me.

But what to do?

***

As I almost had the thought, a possibility occurred. The fact that I even remotely considered it shows how desperate I was. Audrey called.

"Are you ready yet?"

"Am I ready for what?"

"Are you ready to let me back into your life?"

"Why do you keep bothering me Audrey?"

"Because I love you, Rob. I've told you and told you that. Why you won't believe me I'll never understand."

"It should be very easy for you to understand, Audrey. Just think back to that day in the living room when you stood up and said, 'Good.

Now we can get this over with.' Remember that, Audrey? Remember your next words? I believe they were, 'I'm leaving you.' Remember that?"

"I screwed up, Rob. I admitted that I screwed up. I also said that I would take a lie detector test on the cheating and the money. Give me a chance, Rob. Let me prove to you that I love you and want to be with you."

"A chance? Just how bad do you want that chance?"

"I'll do anything Rob, anything at all."

"I doubt that, Audrey, but I guess we will just have to see."

"You'll do it? You'll give me a chance?"

"We need to talk, Audrey, and not on the phone. Meet me at Augie's tomorrow night at six, and we will talk."

Audrey was there waiting for me in one of the rear booths when I got to Augie's Bar and Grill. One look at her and I remembered why I had gone after her in the first place. She really was a very sexy-looking and a very good-looking woman. I sat down across her, and the waitress was there almost immediately. I ordered drinks. When she had taken our order and gone away, I went right to it.

"You hurt me, Audrey. What you did cut me to the quick. Whatever your reason was for doing it doesn't mean a shit to me. What matters to me is what you did to me. You were only thinking of yourself and you didn't give a rat's ass on what it would do to me. You just didn't care and I can't forget that. I don't trust you, Audrey, and that is the reason that I have never considered taking you back. I don't trust you not to break off with me again. You can promise me all your love and devotion for the rest of your life, but you already did that once, remember? When I slid that ring onto your finger? Promise all you want,

Audrey, but I will always be watching and waiting for you to screw me out again.

"The problem is that I am between a rock and a hard place. Letting you back into my life might just be the lesser of two evils. The fact that I'm even considering it shows just how bad things are."

I went on to explain the situation with Kari's daughters.

"I promised her that I would take care of them and I will, but I need to protect myself from them. The only way to do that is to have a woman in my life and bedroom. Given how bold the twins have been in the past, I don't think I have the luxury of taking the time to date and woo a woman. I need something to happen right now."

"Count me in, Rob."

"You haven't heard the whole deal yet, Audrey. You can move back into the house and back into my bedroom, but all we will be doing is putting on a show for the girls. I doubt there will be any sex for a while if ever. I don't know if I can bring myself to touch you."

"It will happen, Rob. I love you and I know that deep inside, you still care for me. I'll bring it out, Rob."

"There is more for you to consider. Are you ready to try and handle two grown girls? Two girls who are going to resent you for taking what they hoped would be theirs? Two girls who are not going to be happy with an adult female filling their recently departed mother's slot in the house?"

"I can handle it, Rob. I can and will do anything I have to do to get you back."

"You have a long, hard road ahead of you, Audrey. The one thing you need to know is that if you and the girls can't get along, you will be the one leaving not them. I promised Kari I would take care of them and

I will. I don't know if I will ever get to the point where I can trust you again, but if you want the shot, I'll give it to you."

"I want it, Rob, and I promise you that you will never be sorry."

"I guess we will find out. When do you want to move back in?"

"Now. I'll start moving my things as soon as we leave here."

"No, Audrey. I have to talk with Bev and Barb first. Nothing they will say will change anything, but I do owe them an advanced notice. You can move back in tomorrow."

Tears were running down her cheeks as she said, "Thank you, Rob, thank you."

***

Driving home, I wondered if it would work. God knew that I still had strong feelings for Audrey. There was a fine line between love and hate, and on any given day, I could be found on one side of that line or the other. Before Kari moved into my bedroom, I'd wake up missing Audrey and wishing that she was there on the bed beside me. Then, I would remember just why she wasn't there and I'd cross over to the other side of the line. Even after Kari became my full time bed buddy, I'd think of Audrey during the day at work and wonder where she was and what she was doing. Then, I'd remember what she'd done and be back on the bad side of the line.

Would it work? I had no idea but I hoped that it would at least long enough for the girls to find steady boyfriends. They dated a lot but neither of them had come up with a special guy.

When I walked into the house, I heard Bev on the phone. "I don't know? I'll have to ask my dad." That stopped me dead in my tracks. It was the first time I heard either of them refer to me as dad. It suddenly occurred to me just how much trust Kari had in me when she made me promise to take care of her girls. It was a pretty humbling experience.

"I'm home," I called out as I closed the door behind me.

Dinner was ready. As we sat down to eat, I wondered if I would still be called dad after I talk with them. I knew I couldn't put it off, so as soon as we finished, dinner I said:

"We need to talk."

"About what?" asked Barb.

"About what is going to happen around here. As you both know your mother and I had an arrangement. What you don't know," I lied, "is that the arrangement was about to change. Your mother was in the process of moving back into her room when the bad shit happened."

"Why?" asked Bev, "why would she do that? She was happy with the way things were."

I kept the lie going. "Your mother knew that what we had was never going to be long term. She knew I was still in love with my wife. She never understood why, especially knowing what Audrey had done to me, but she did know that I was still in love with Audrey. Audrey and I have been talking and trying to work things out, and we decided to get back together and see if we could make things work. Your mother was moving so Audrey could move back in. Because of what happened, we put off Audrey's move to let things settle down a bit around here. I wanted to give you a little advance notice that is why I brought it up tonight. Audrey will be moving back in tomorrow."

"How could you!" Bev cried, "Didn't mom mean anything to you at all?"

"Your mother meant a great deal to me, honey; but your mother didn't love me, and I didn't love her. It is like I said, we had an arrangement. You never knew, at least I don't think you did, but that arrangement came about because of you."

I told them about their mother overhearing their plans for me and how she decided that the only way to prevent it from happening was to get to me first. "So, it started out just as a way to keep you two away from me. Over time we developed feelings for each other, but those feelings were never more than a strong affection for each other. We were very good friends, friends with benefits as it were, but still just friends."

"What about us?" Barb wanted to know.

"Nothing changes as far as you two are concerned. Your mother gave you to me, and I promised her that I would take care of you. You are mine now. Audrey is not coming here to become a replacement mother for you. I am hoping you will be able to get along and in time become friends, but if it doesn't happen it doesn't happen. But you need to know that this is your home and that is not going to change. You are my girls now, and that is the bottom line."

Both girls looked at me, and then Barb showed that she was a little savvier than I credited her for.

"Is this you getting together with your wife to try and put things back together, or is this just another arrangement being put in place to keep Bev and me out of your bedroom? Be honest with us here, daddy. If you say that this is just a way to hold us at bay, you really don't have to do it. I will promise to behave and leave you be rather than to see you do something you really don't want to do."

"Me too, daddy." Bev said, "Please don't do it if you really don't want to."

Well, there it was: my way out. I knew that if the twins promised me something, they would follow through with it. The problem was the timing. If I had the conversation with them the night before—after I set the time to meet Audrey but before meeting her—things might have gone differently because I would have had their promise; but I didn't have the talk so I didn't have the promise when Audrey and I had our sit down. What I did have was that Kari and her friend Matty told me that Audrey had never engaged in sex when she spent her time running around with Anna and the Diablos. A Audrey had also volunteered to take a lie detector test on the subject. I pretty much accepted that she hadn't cheated on me before leaving me. After? Who knows?

Audrey was a healthy woman with a healthy woman's sexual appetite. Because I wouldn't let her come back, I really couldn't blame her if she found someone to scratch her itch especially since I was busy letting Kari scratch mine. The fact was that I was ready to let Audrey come home. I was ready to try and put things back together. Would it help where Bev and Barb were concerned? Probably, but I did have to admit to myself that I did want to try it again with Audrey.

I looked from Bev to Barb and asked, "When did you start calling me daddy?"

"Months and months ago," Bev said. "We always referred to you as dad when we talked to mom and our friends. We never said it to you because we didn't know if you would like it."

"Thank you, both. I'm honored that you think so well of me. Now, to answer your question: I am taking Audrey back because I want to see if we can put our marriage back together. In fact it was your mom who helped convince me that Audrey never cheated on me. My thinking that she had cheated was the big reason that kept us from getting back together."

Of course they didn't know, and I was never going to let them know that my getting back with Audrey had indeed started out as an arrangement to protect me from them.

"Okay, daddy" Bev said, "If you are sure that is what you want to do, we will try to like her but it will be hard."

"Why?"

"Oh come on, dad" Bev said, "You know we both still want to climb on your bed, and your wife will be on the way."

"Why won't the two of you accept that it is never going to happen?"

Barb chuckled and said, "Never is a long time daddy, and over time things can change."

"Well little girl, one thing that hasn't changed is that dinner clean-up is still your job so get to it."

I didn't get much sleep that night. In my mind was the thought that the twins knew Audrey would be moving back in the next day. They might see that because I would be alone that night, it might be a good time to take a shot at me. I remembered their plan that brought their mother into my bed. Every little noise had me looking at the bedroom door, but morning came without my having to fight them off.

***

When I got home from work that night, I found that Audrey had taken a day off from work and had used that day to move back into the house. She and the girls were in the kitchen, making dinner. Because they weren't scowling at each other, I assumed that things were okay so far.

Barb said, "Dinner will be ready in about five minutes, daddy." I saw Audrey gave a quick glance at Barb's way. I would bet that that daddy was Barb's way of letting Audrey know she was staking a claim to a part of me and that there was a strong relationship that Audrey wasn't going to be allowed to mess with.

Dinner conversation was mostly Audrey and the girls getting to know each other. Audrey wanted to know about what they liked in school, did they have boyfriends, what they wanted to do when they got out of school, and other stuff like that. The twins wanted to know about Audrey, and in the process, I found out about things I hadn't known. Before the split, Audrey had worked part time in a clothing store. While she was gone, she had taken classes at the community college, had gotten a full time job as a legal secretary, and was still taking classes to become a paralegal. The three women seemed to like each other enough to get along, and that is all I cared about.

The girls were off doing their homework, and Audrey and I were sitting on the couch in the living room when she said:

"Daddy? They call you daddy?"

"I had no say on the matter, Aud. It is what they decided they wanted to call me."

"Still, I have a hard time seeing you as a daddy."

"It is just a term of affection, Aud not a description of what or who I am. As what Kari once told me, they have always wanted a father figure in their lives and I guess they decided that it was going to be me."

"I think I like them, Rob, and I hope they like me."

That night when we went to bed, I was wearing pajamas. I usually sleep naked, so it was my way of letting Audrey knew there was not going to have any sex. When she got on bed she moved over to snuggle up to me, and I moved away from her. She rolled over her side and we both went to sleep.

I woke up with a hot mouth on my dick and in my half asleep half-awake state, I thought it was Kari. Then I remembered that she was gone. I thought Bev or Barb must have come into the room. I was all set to panic when I remembered Audrey was there. By the time I had worked it all out in my head, Audrey had impaled herself on my cock and was riding me. I tensed and Audrey hissed:

"Don't even think about it. Try to push me away and I'll sink my nails so deep into you. I'll tear chunks out of you as you push me off."

She need not to bother with the threat because by then, the little head had taken control over the big head.

"It has been too damned long for me, baby. Tomorrow, we can make love but tonight we fuck."

And we did it three times. Audrey wanted a fourth, but I could not get it back up. She tried though. She spent twenty minutes with her mouth on me, but it would just not get up to play. Finally, she looked down at me and said:

"You, bastard! You were fucking Kari, weren't you?

I just shrugged and she went on, "No way! You could have lasted as long as you did if you had gone without since I've been gone."

Again, all I could do was shrug.

"Not fair. If Kari would have been honest with me, I might have been able to play a little too and I would have not suffered so much. Not fair at all."

***

Over the next month, Audrey did her best to try and make up for the lost time. We had two and sometimes three times every night and I would go to work in the morning exhausted. Finally, she must have figured that she had caught up enough to back off a bit. The love making slacked off to three or four times a week and usually only once a night.

Audrey and the twins had settled into a sisterly relationship with Audrey being the big sister. Together, they went shopping for clothes and Audrey took them to the beauty parlor she went to. It was the twin's first visit to a hair dresser, and they couldn't wait to get home and show me their new hair style. Yes, style, not styles. They were still doing the twin thing and trying to stay alike.

It was coming up: the twin's eighteenth birthday and graduation was going to be on the same week. The girls earned some scholarships and they both planned on attending the community college to study Nursing degrees. Audrey was still taking evening classes—three nights a week—to get what she needed to become a paralegal. The girls were pumping her about what college was like. Audrey tried to talk them into attending a regular school for nursing, but the girls insisted on going for the community college route. It seemed to upset Audrey, but I didn't think anything of it at that time.

Audrey decided to throw a combination-of-birthday-and-graduation party for them. The house was full of kids and I was kept busy making sure that nothing would get the police or other parents involved. I caught the kids twice sneaking away to drink from a bottle they had stashed. I also had to chase a couple out of one of the bedrooms. But all in all, it was a good party.

Audrey and I were in the kitchen cleaning up when Barb came in to help.

"Where's Bev?" I asked.

"She and Marv are on the swing in the back yard, necking. I don't know what she sees in him. He is such a twit."

Audrey giggled and said, "Twits need loving too."

"She probably thinks the same about Randy," I said.

"Oh, puleease." Barb snorted, "Randy is just a date, and I don't have any interest in him."

"Is that why you sat in his car steaming up the windows when he brought you home last night?"

"I didn't say that I didn't like him, just that he is nobody special."

"Right!" Audrey and I said almost in unison.

***

The twins got jobs for the summer. The months flew by and the girls were off to college. Before the month was out, Bev had come up with a steady boyfriend, and for the first time since I met them, they were spending much more time apart. Barb seemed contented to play the field.

Audrey was working hard trying to prove to me that I was the love of her life; but as I told her before she moved back in, getting my trust back was going to be a hard thing for her to do. I watched her for any sign that wasn't as it should be. She had evening classes on Monday, Wednesday, and Thursday. One Wednesday, I parked down the street from where she worked and followed her to see where she went after work. She drove to the college, got out of her car with a book bag, and walked into one of the buildings.

The holidays came around and with them were the usual parties. Audrey and I had a good time at my company Christmas party, but I couldn't say the same for hers. I got the definite impression from the people she worked with that as a production line supervisor I was beneath them. When Audrey introduced me to the lawyer for whom she was working as a secretary, I disliked the man instantaneously. I can't explain why but I did not like him. Maybe it was the way he looked at me or maybe it was his hand shake, but I knew right away that I didn't like and would never like Mark Hathaway. I did my best to be sociable for Audrey's sake, but I was more than happy to say goodnight to the bunch when the party broke up.

At the dinner table during the Christmas Eve, Bev asked, "Does anybody notice anything different?" as she patted her hair with her left hand. I didn't catch it, but Audrey did and shortly after she said, "Oh my God!" Barb squealed, "When?"

"Yesterday," Bev said as she stuck her hand out to show off the engagement ring. "Benny proposed last night when he brought me home. We aren't going to get married until I get my degree, but Benny said he had to ask now before someone else beat him to it."

Barb and Audrey started with the questions: Did he go down on his knee? What did he say? Were you surprised? And on and on. I got up and left the three of them there yakking away.

***

It was a Wednesday in February —the day before Valentine's Day. Bev was out somewhere with Benny. Audrey was at her Wednesday night class. Barb and I were at home, alone.

"Can I ask you something personal, dad?"

"Sure you can, sweetie, but I may not answer you."

"Is everything okay between you and Audrey?"

"As far as I know. Why do you ask?"

"Just curious."

"Bullshit, baby girl. You don't ask anything for no reason. What prompted that question?"

"I'm sorry I asked. It isn't any of my business anyway."

"But you did ask, Barb so give in."

"It is just that Audrey is supposed to be taking evening classes like I am, but I never see her there. The place isn't so big that we shouldn't run into each other every once in a while."

"I don't know why you never see each other. But to answer your question, everything is fine with us."

At least I thought it was, but was it?

Thursday, I parked down the street from the law offices of Bingham, Bingham and Hathaway (BB and H) when Audrey came out the front door in the arms of Mark Hathaway. They got into his Cadillac Escalade and drove off. I followed them. They drove to a gated community near the country club. I had no way to follow them inside so I parked where I could watch the gate. Three hours later, the Escalade came out. I followed it back to the BB and H employee lot. Audrey got out of the car, leaned back inside, gave Hathaway a kiss, and then walked to her car.

I shot home. I was there sitting on the couch, watching TV when she got home. She breezed in, kissed me, and told me that it had been a rough day at work followed by a bad night at school. One of her instructors picked the paper she just turned in to pieces.

"I'm going to go soak in the tub and then we can go to bed where you can console me. Sound like a plan?"

I wasn't quite ready to confront her so I just smiled and said, "You bet." I managed to get through the weekend without strangling her.

On Monday, I followed her and Hathaway again. On Wednesday, she did actually go to school. But on Thursday, they were back to the gated community again. I knew all I needed to know so I drove home and began to make plans.

Audrey was history and that was given. However, I needed a way to get back at Hathaway so I was stuck with pretending that all was well with Audrey and me until I could come up with a plan. Over the next two weeks I came up with a dozen plans, but every one of them turned out to have a glitch. I could have just caught Hathaway alone somewhere and stomped the fuck out of him, but it isn't what I wanted. I wanted to ruin him. I wanted to sue him for alienation of affection and smear his reputation as a lawyer. Maybe I should do enough good job so that his partners would kick him out of the firm. To get what I needed though, I needed a way to get into his gated community so I could peek in his windows and take photos, or kick down his door and get pictures of Audrey and him doing the dirty.

I made an appointment with a private detective. He told me that there wasn't any way I could get what I really needed. He said he could arrange to be inside the gate when Hathaway and Audrey got there and take pictures of Audrey going inside the town home, but those pictures would prove nothing other than Audrey had visited. Even if he could get inside Hathaway's place and plant video cameras and recording devices, their product would be inadmissible as evidence because they would have been illegally obtained. His advice to me was to suck it up, sue using irreconcilable differences, and be done with it.

I was sitting on the couch with a beer in my hand, staring at the wall and trying to think of some way to fuck Hathaway when Audrey came into the room and sat down beside me.

"Where are you right now?"

"What?"

"You have been distant lately. And here you are sitting, staring at the wall. So where are you right now? Where is your head?"

I didn't say anything, just looked at her. She reached over and touched me.

"You know, don't you?"

I looked at her and nodded my head "yes."

"The girls are going on a ski trip with some friends this weekend. I was going to tell you then while we were alone, but I guess now is as good as any other time. I love you, Rob. I really and truly do, but it isn't working out. It isn't your fault. I am the one who made it so you would never trust me again. The ironic part is that even though I never did what made you distrust me in the first place, you were right in not trusting me when I came back.

"I really did want to put us back together. I have tried my damnedest since I've been back, but it hasn't gotten me anywhere and I've come to realize that it never will. We have sex, but you have never really made love to me since I've been back and we don't snuggle and cuddle like we used to. You barely show me any affection at all. In a way, you are to blame for what has been going on because you are the one who kept pounding it home that you doubted we would ever make it. I came home with high hopes. But in the back of my mind, I always doubted that you would ever accept me again. I convinced myself that the only reason you let me come back was so that I could be your protection against the girls.

"I lied and I am sure you know I did when I said I had never had sex while we were apart. I never did before I left, but I couldn't go without it forever. I started an affair with Mark about three months after I started working for the firm. It was supposed to be just friends with benefits kind of thing at first. I told him up front that I still loved you and intended to get back with you somehow. He accepted that and even tried to help. He was the one who suggested the trial separation to force counseling, but we know how that turned out. Over the course of our relationship, Mark fell in love with me. I liked him. I liked him a lot, but my level of affection for him wasn't anywhere close to how I felt about you. I made it plain to Mark that you were my guy. He loved me enough to want to see me happy, so he accepted that I was always going to want you first and he accepted what little I would give him.

"Then, we talked. You agreed to let me come home, and that is where I failed you. No matter how much I loved you and no matter how bad I wanted it to work out, I didn't think that it would because you constantly tell me how hard it would be for you to ever trust me again. So I hung on to Mark as my security blanket. I would meet him once a week or so to keep him interested in me. I really did have classes during night as I said I did. Six weeks ago, I tested out of my Monday and Thursday classes. Last month, I finally accepted that you and I were never going to be any more than friendly roommates. Being friendly roommates isn't just enough for me, Rob. I love you too much to just settle for that. I started spending my now freed up Mondays and Thursdays with Mark, thinking about what I should do. I decided to do both of us a favor and end it.

"I'm going to file divorce for irreconcilable differences, and Mark is going to handle it for me. I won't be asking for anything except the end of the marriage. After a suitable length of time, I will most likely marry Mark. I know I will never love him as deeply as I've loved you, but at least he wants me—all of me. I'm sorry it didn't work out, Rob. God knows I would have given anything to make it work, but I guess some things are not just meant to be."

She leaned over, kissed me, and said, "I'll sleep in the spare bedroom tonight and move out while you are at work tomorrow."

She got up and left the room, but paused at the stairs and said, "Don't ever doubt it, Rob. I do love you," and then she went up the stairs. She was gone when I got home from work the next day.

***

It happened just as she said. It was served and she asked for nothing. I didn't even have to get an attorney. All I had to do was sign the papers and send them back—that's all, just sign them and send them back—but for some strange reason, I didn't do it. I tossed the papers on the desk in the den and left them lay there.

In the next week, the twins tried to cheer me up by telling me that it was all for the best, that it was obvious it was never going to work out, that it was never meant to be, and other such platitudes. One night, I woke up as someone climbed into bed with me.

I heard Barb's voice saying, "Relax, daddy. Your pee-pee is safe. I just thought you needed someone to hold you, and I appointed myself as the holder."

We fell asleep in each other's arms. The next night, it was Bev. The night after that, it was Barb again. For the next week the girls rotated and surprisingly enough, they behaved.

Until one Monday morning…

I woke up with Barb's hand on my cock. I went to push it away, but she held on to it.

"I told you the other night that your pee-pee was safe, but I had to let you know that I still want it. I'm over eighteen, daddy, and I'm totally legal. I dearly want what I have in my hand, but you have to be the one to make it happen. There won't be any sneak attacks from me: no ropes around the chair, no waking you up with blow jobs in the middle of the night. I'm yours if you want me, but you will have to be the one to make it happen."

She let go of my cock, kissed me, and then said, "I've got until eight o'clock this morning and I'm going to have to hurry to make it." She got up and left the room, leaving me with a seriously hard dick.

Barb and Bev were indeed both legal and they had both wanted to be in my bed. I didn't know about Bev now that she was engaged to Benny, but it was obvious that Barb was ready.

One thing I had never done was lie to myself. I had lusted after both of the girls since the day Kari had brought them to the house. It was only my determination not to go to jail as a child molester that had kept me away from them. That fear was now gone, but something else had taken its place. That night when Barb came home, I told her flat out that what she wanted could never be.

"You are of legal age, sweetie. I will admit that I have always wanted you, but there is something in the way. Even though there are no blood ties between us, you are my daughter. Your mother in her dying breath entrusted you to me. I promised her that I would take care of you. I was aware that what she was asking of me was that I keep you safe. To me, that meant safe from all harm and safe from what your mother feared most—that you and I or Bev and I would have sex. Your mom was so dead set against it ever happening that she put herself on my bed to keep you out of it. I will not betray your mother's trust. You are my girl, my baby, and my daughter; as such, I will never touch you in the way you want. I will love you and cherish you as a father should, and that will have to be enough for you."

Tears started flowing and she cried out, "that's just not fair" as she ran from the room. As I watched her go, I thought, *Maybe not fair baby girl, but it is what's right.*

***

Audrey was surprised when she came out of the BB and H office with Hathaway to find me sitting on a folding chair in the sidewalk. I pointed to the other folding chair and said, "Sit!" She looked from me to Mark and then back at me; and then she sat down. I handed her the divorce papers and said:

"If you look at it, you will see that they are not signed. Before you ask me why, I have a few things to say. I cheated on you when I told you that you could come back and try to put things back together. I let you come back but all the while, I had the thought in the back of my mind that it was never going to happen. I had already made up my mind that you were going to leave me again in your search for fun and excitement, and why wouldn't you? I was an unexciting stick in the mud. I knew it. —I also knew that's who I was, and I wasn't going to change.

Not really believing we had a chance, I didn't try. I went through the motions with one eye on the calendar trying to pick out the day, week, or month when it would happen. What is so stupid about it is that I really did want it to work. I did want us to put things back together.

"Everyone knows that the brain needs oxygen to function properly. I had my head so far up my ass where you were concerned that my brain wasn't getting any oxygen. When Barb tipped me out that you weren't at school on Mondays and Thursdays, I followed you and saw where you went. I remembered when you first came home and how upset you seemed to get when the girls said no to a regular nursing school and insisted on going the community college route. I figured it was because you were afraid they would find out that you didn't really take classes, and they would tell me. Following you to Hathaway's confirmed that you had been fucking him all along. That made me believe—along with my not believing we could make it—that you weren't even intending to try. You were playing some kind of game—setting me up so you could leave me in some nasty way—to get even with me for tossing you out. Why else would you be wasting your time with me and spending your evenings with your boyfriend here?"

Hathaway gave me a nasty look. Audrey started to say something, but I held up my hand to cut her off.

"Let me finish, and then you can have your say. On your last day, you said that you would have given anything to make it work. The sad thing is that, even though I wanted it to work, I gave nothing. So here it is, Audrey. I am willing to give everything and do anything to try and make it work. I have no way of knowing if you still feel that way. You have the divorce papers in your hand. Take them with you and think about them. If they show up in my mailbox in a day or so, I will sign them and send them back."

I stood up and turned to go. I hadn't taken three steps when Audrey called my name. I turned. She held the divorce papers up in front of her, tore them in half, dropped them on the ground, and then ran to me. As I held her, Hathaway walked up and said:

"If you hurt her, you will answer to me."

I looked at him for a couple of seconds; and then I smiled and said, "I could almost learn to like you."

The End

Here is a sample from another story you may enjoy:

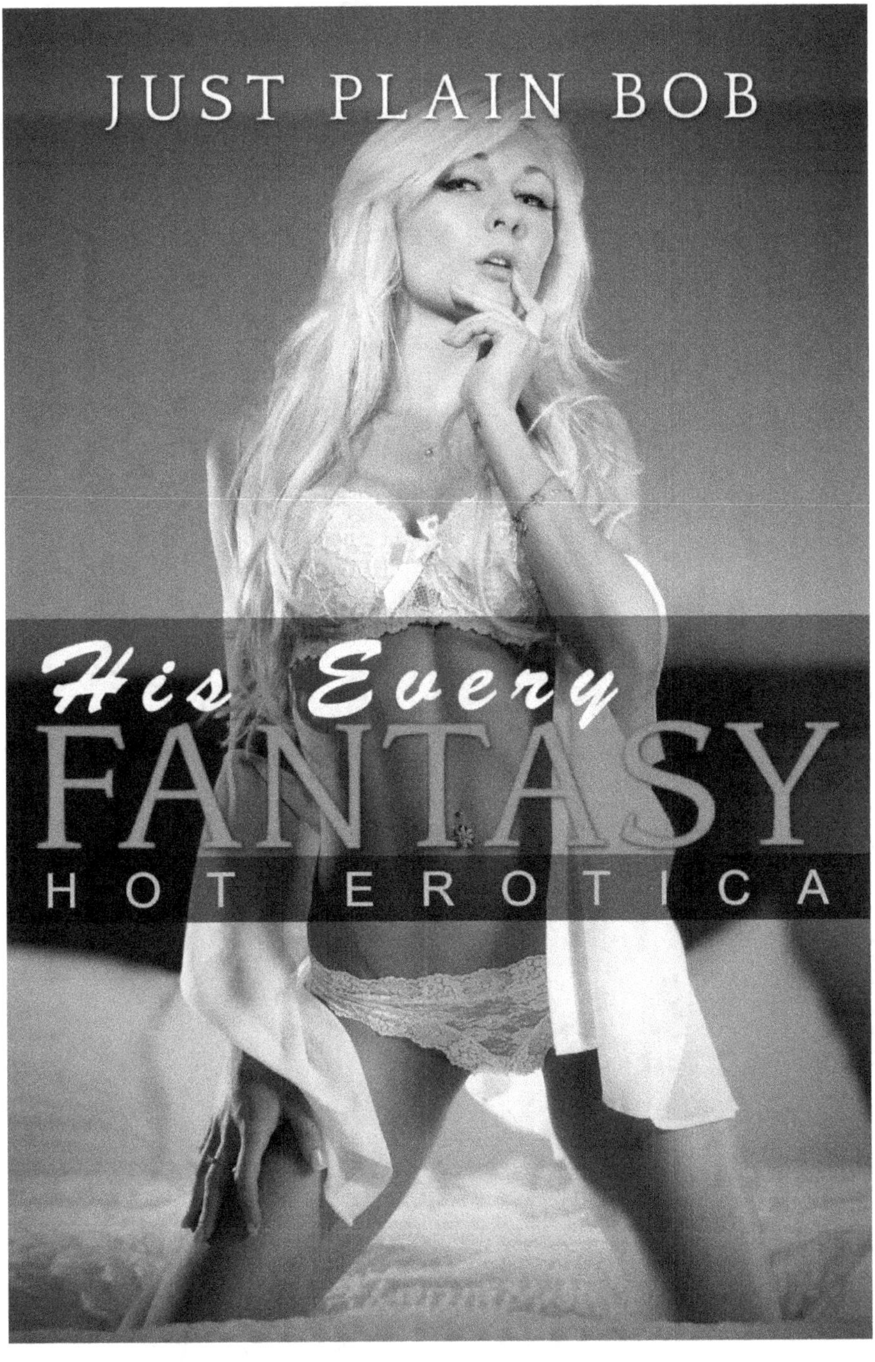
JUST PLAIN BOB
His Every
FANTASY
HOT EROTICA

Everyone has fantasies. Some are sexual, some are financial and some are about fame. One guy's fantasy might be to be the quarterback that leads his team into the Super Bowl and another guy's might be to pitch the only really perfect game – 27 batters and 27 strike outs – in the World Series. I used to work with a guy whose fantasy was to find a lamp at an antique store, rub it and have a genie appear so he could wish for a ten-inch dick. And of course, everyone fantasizes about what they would do if they hit the 217 million dollar Power Ball lottery.

My fantasy was to be stranded on a deserted island with porn star Kristal Summers or be walking down a street and have a car pull over and a voice call out "Hey you!" I turn and see Kristal looking out the window smiling as she says, "I want you to be in my next video." Or a knock on my door some night and when I answer it I find Kristal standing there. "My car broke down in front of your place. Can you help me?" Or….oh well, you get the idea.

I found her one night while I was surfing porn sites on the Net and one look at that face and she had me. I have downloaded 11 videos of her and I am constantly looking for more. I spend more time on the computer than is good for me, but I don't have anything else to do. No, that isn't really true. There is a lot I could get out and do, but I have lost the desire to do any of it. If I left my computer and ventured out I would run into friends and friends being what they are they would try and cheer me up. Tell me that it was probably for the best and some would try to play matchmaker and fix me up with "this girl who is absolutely perfect for you."

And that is what I am afraid of. Another girl who is perfect for me. I've already had two girls who were "absolutely perfect for me" and between the two of them, they managed to rip my heart out.

The first one was Annalise. A five-foot, two-inch blond bombshell. At 36x23x34, she was a walking wet dream who stunned the hell out of me when she walked up to me at a party and said:

"The idiot who brought me to this party is a real drag. How about you take me out of here and we go find some place where we can have a few drinks, dance a little and get to know each other."

I might have been a little tongue-tied, but I wasn't stupid and I offered her my arm and we left the party. We went to the Starlight Lounge and drank, danced and talked and I found out that she was 24, a legal secretary, lived alone in an apartment on Sudsbury Avenue and that her favorite color was blue. She had no hometown loyalties; her favorite football team was the Cowboys, favorite baseball team was the Bluejays, the Red Wings were her hockey team and she had absolutely no interest in basketball.

"Those ugly tattoos they cover themselves with are absolutely disgusting."

She liked opera, ballet, classical music, bluegrass and hated 'rap' music. I wanted to ask her why she picked me, but I was afraid to. She might have said:

"I don't know, but now that we are here I don't think that it was such a good idea."

The week before the wedding, I had a bachelor party and her girlfriends took her out for a bachelorette party. Mine was predictable. Some drinking, some card playing and about eleven o'clock a stripper arrived. She was fairly good looking and her dance and the lap dance that followed were okay, but didn't do a thing for me. Why would it? I had 'sex bomb' Annalise at home. I was asleep when Annalise got home and she was dead to the world when I got up to go to work in the morning.

Two days later, I received an envelope in the mail at work and when I opened it I found five things. A note that said "Are you sure that you want to marry this?" and four photos of Annalise being enjoyed sexually by at least six different men. In one picture she had a cock in her mouth, ass and pussy and in another she had her hand – left one with engagement ring showing – guiding a large cock into her mouth.

If you enjoyed this sample then look for **His Every Fantasy.**

Here is another preview of a story that you may also enjoy:

The narrow village road looked the same. Nothing had changed since she left a few years ago. Time had left her home village behind. There were no new houses and the old ones were just as she remembered them, each set back away from the road and surrounded by flowering bushes and fruit trees.

No one was out and about at this time of day. Most of the villagers would be tending their vegetable plots and rice fields. Anna walked to a small wooden house raised five feet above the ground on short, stout timber beams.

She took off her shoes and using the dipper, scooped water from the big urn next to the steps and washed her feet, the way all the villagers did before entering their homes.

She climbed up the six steps, crossed the small verandah to the closed door. It was not locked. None of the villagers had cause to lock their homes. Everyone knew everybody and strangers never pass their way. It was as if their village had been forgotten and it remained as it had always been. Simple wooden houses were built raised off the ground in case the heavy monsoon rains caused the small stream running by the village to overflow and flood the surroundings. There were no fences, only well-worn paths leading off to the twenty or so homes, each well-tended and boasting a variety of flowering shrubs, potted plants and fruit trees.

Anna walked into the small living room. All was quiet except for the cat that purred, opening her eyes as she sensed Anna.

"Putih!" Anna called out and the cat padded over to her, rubbing its head against Anna's bare ankles.

Anna carried her small suitcase into the back room. It had not changed. The single bed with a dresser next to the window, was neatly made. The wooden chair beside the bed was still there. On it sat the cushion embroidered with a prowling tiger. The tiger stared at her, its eyes probing her innermost secrets. The cushion was one of a set of two. She had bought the set as the tiger embodied a life-changing experience for her and Song. She had given the other cushion to Song as a potent reminder of how close they came to be a meal for the tiger. Song, his name threatened to push her into places she had no wish to revisit.

She had come home. This was the room of her childhood and adolescence, her refuge from the storms that had ripped her life apart at a tender age. Her grandparents had taken her in and raised her in this little village ever since she was five.

She looked at the photographs hanging on the wall. There were three altogether.

One showed Anna as a young child with her parents, Zul and Ainee.

The second showed Anna in school uniform clutching a trophy, flanked by her beaming grandparents.

The third showed Anna alone, with the iconic Petronas Twin Towers of Kuala Lumpur in the background.

Her life history depicted by these three photographs left big blanks that strained the curiosity of those who had come to know Anna and visited her village home.

The dream did not fade over time, not like her grandma had said it would. She used to wake up screaming, cowering in fear and her grandma would rush in and hold her, rocking her gently, murmuring words of love and assurance until her sobs subsided into hiccups and she fell asleep in Grandma's arms.

As she grew older, she learned to stifle her screams with her pillow and not wake her grandparents because they had to get up early to tend to their rice field about half a kilometer away from their village.

The first photograph triggered sketchy memories of her parents.

Her mother was a beautiful woman with big flashing eyes and red lips that often parted in a wide smile. Her father was short, like her grandfather, but had broad shoulders. Anna remembered his strong arms whenever he lifted her into the air and she would scream in delight. She also remembered the big fights whenever mama came home late and there was no dinner on the table for papa, no dinner for Anna, who had been alone in the flat when papa unlocked the front door.

If you enjoy this sample then look for **The Red Peony by Denise Denton**.

Also by this Author:

The Prodigal Family: The Abbotts

Watching My Shared Wife

The Waitress and the Runaway Husband

Baiting Mr. Little

Too Hot for Henry

Chuck's Fantasy

Wife Sharing and Other Adventures

The Redhead's Desires

Rescued at Riley's

Hazardous Wives

Wives Who Stray

His Every Fantasy

Open Mike Night

Pursuit for Revenge

Why Does He Do That?

Halloween & Drugs

From the Author

If you enjoyed any of my books then please share the love and promote my books in Amazon.

If you write me a review and send me an email I will send you a free book, or many.
(Just know that these emails are filtered by my publisher.)

Good news is always welcome.

One Last Thing, For Kindle Readers...

When you turn the page, Kindle will give you the opportunity to rate this book and share your thoughts on Facebook and Twitter. If you enjoyed my writings, would you please take a few seconds to let your friends know about it? Because... when they enjoy they will be grateful to you and so will I.

Thank You!

An Open Letter from Just Plain Bob

A message for those who like my stories, those who hate my stories, those who are indifferent and those who have yet to make up their minds.

I have often stated that I really don't care what others think about my stories, that I write for my own enjoyment and then I offer to share. If you like my stories fine and if you don't, also fine since I have already satisfied my target audience - me!

It is human nature to strive to get better. If you take up bowling your first games are going low scoring, but you will work and practice to get better and as your average climbs you may forget the game where you had three gutter balls and shot an eighty-six, but that game is still there in your past.

Your first time on the golf course you shot an eighty on the front nine, but did you settle for that being your game or did you work to improve? You may eventually get a three handicap, but that nine hole eighty is still there as part of your past.

When you hired in at your job did you say, "Cool, I got it made" and do nothing more than what you barely had to do or did you go to work thinking that, "Someday I'm going to be running this place." You might never climb that high, but human nature says that you are going to at least try.

It is the same with authors who write stories and post them on sites like Literotica. Their first stories might not be all that good, but comments and feedback along with a desire to get better drive them toward putting out a better product or to at least try.

I'm no different. My first stories might not have been all that great, but they are still there on the hard drive. I like cheating wife stories and five years ago I found my first adult site that catered to cheating wife stories. It was a pay site, but it had a policy of giving a free lifetime membership to anyone who submitted five stories to the site. How hard can that be I said to myself as I sat down and fired up the word processor and went to work.

I sent my five stories in and sat back to enjoy my free membership and a funny thing happened. I started getting feedback, most of it positive, and I became hooked. I started cranking out more stories. The site I was sending my stories to had seven categories:

Bisexual
Cream Pie

Groups
I Watch
Gang Bang
Racial
SM/BD

I know nothing about bisexual or SM/BD and I had no interest in Groups so all the stories I wrote I tailored for the four remaining categories:

Cream Pie
I Watch
Gang Bang
Racial.

I turned out eight stories a month, two for each category, which means that after five years I have over 120 stories in each of those categories and they are all still on the hard drive.

A year ago I received an email asking me why I never posted stories on Literotica. The answer? I didn't know about Lit. I pulled it up, liked what I saw, and started sending in stories to it. All new stories? No, not hardly, not with over 400 stories sitting on the hard drive. Maybe one new story for each fifteen or so old ones. The newer ones are better, at least I think they are and I have received some feedback that leads me to believe that others think so too, and I will continue to write new ones.

But I am still going to recycle what is on the hard drive, stories that were written specifically to fit the four categories. That means that those of you who hate cream pie stories still have eighty or so to look forward to. Ditto for those who call me a racist; you will get another seventy or so interracial stories.

Those who hate wimps will only see about fifty more of those because the stories I sent to the I Watch category were split 50/50 between what some call wimps and some call "real men." Why the 50/50 split? It came from listening to the readers. I would get feedback asking me why all the men in my stories were hard asses. "In real life men are more forgiving, especially if it is the first indiscretion." So I would write stories with forgiving husbands and boyfriends and then the next batch of feedback would say, "Why are all your husbands spineless wimps" and I'd write stories that went back the other way.

Eventually I came to realize that I was wasting my time - there was no way I could write a story that would satisfy everybody and that is when I adopted my philosophy of writing for my own enjoyment and then offering to share.

As far as the gangbang stories? Well, what can I say? Gangbangs are gangbangs and there are still eighty or so of them to go.

The bottom line is that Literotica readers are going to see more of my old stories than my new ones. If I'm still around three or four years from now it will probably go the other way, more new than old.

I feel the need to respond to some of the comments and emails I have received. By far the largest percentage comes from people who say, "You are an asshole because all women are not whores and sluts and that's all you make them out to be."

Next most common is, "You must really hate women you sick fuck."

"You must be a wimp because all the men in your stories are wimps" is up there in the top ten along with, "Why don't you give it a rest and go crawl off in a hole somewhere."

There is a lot more, but I'm only going to address those four and in reverse order.

I won't stop and go crawl in a hole because I am enjoying the hell out of what I am doing and remember what I said, I am doing this for MY OWN ENJOYMENT and then I offer to share. Some obviously like my sharing with them and so I will continue to do so. No one is holding a gun to a reader's head and telling them they must click on a Just Plain Bob story or die. It is a conscious choice on the reader's part to move that mouse and click on that story.

When a man finds out he has a cheating wife or girlfriend there are only a limited number of ways he can handle it. If he loves her he can forgive, try to forget and try to hold on and somehow make things work. He can turn his back on her, walk away and get on with his life. The third option is to take revenge.

According to a good portion of those who send me feedback the first and second options are proof that the men are wimps. If the man takes the third option he is still considered a wimp if he doesn't do some sort of physical damage to the woman and her lover. These readers believe that the only way not to be a wimp is to kill, maim and destroy everything in sight. Doing that however, will invariably get the man throw in jail and that is why it so rarely happens in real life.

In real life most revenge takes place in the man's head when he says to himself, "I should have _____ (fill in the blank) the fucking cunt!" I know this because I have been there and done that (see The Dark Trilogy). In my stories I try to mirror real life so kill, maim and destroy are going to be for the most part absent. Outside of some fisticuffs there will be very little physical violence in my stories. Most of my husbands are going to do what I did, what several of my friends and others that I know have done, forgive, or walk away. If this makes them wimps and me a wimp for writing the story that way, so be it.

Next is the "I must hate all women." Nothing could be farther from the truth. I love women. I lust after women. I even like whores and sluts. I have been married four times, engaged two other times (that did not end in marriage) and I have always had girlfriends between marriages. My philosophy is that women were put on this earth for me to enjoy and I'm not talking just sexually. I could sit at the mall (and have) for hours and just girl watch.

The engagements, girlfriends and three of the four marriages bring me to the #1 anti JPB comment on the list.

"You are an asshole because all women aren't whores and sluts."

Well dear reader, you can not prove that by me! I will say up front that I KNOW all women aren't whores and sluts, BUT the majority of the women in my life were. My mother ran around on my father for years while he was driving a truck for a living. My Aunt Margaret cheated regularly on my Uncle Bill, as did my Aunt Mildred on my Uncle Paul. My Aunt Betty fucked around on my Uncle Bob for years and finally left him for his brother, my Uncle Wendell. Uncle Wendell in turn caught her on her knees at his company Christmas party giving Season's Greetings to his boss.

My sister is three times divorced and each divorce came about when the then current husband caught her out spreading pollen. Both of the engagements I mentioned ended when I found out that I was not the one and only and a lot of the girls I dated between marriages never made it to engagement status for the same reason.

And that brings me to my three ex-wives. The first one, Helen (I believe I commented on her in the intro to The Dark Trilogy) had seven different lovers before I found out what was going on. I was living proof that love is blind. Ditto with my second wife. She had a secret life that she hid from me and when I found out about her brother, his friends and the gangbangs she was history.

My third marriage ended in divorce because of a different kind of cheating (and I can just imagine the outrage I am going to get over this) - she cheated on me with an idea. I was away from home on business, she was lonely, a couple of Jehovah's Witnesses knocked on the door and my wife, with nothing better to do invited them in. When I came home from my trip I found out that she had found God. On a scale that runs from TRUE BELIEVER on one end to ATHEIST on the other you will find me just to the right of AGNOSTIC and since I would not allow myself to be SAVED the marriage eventually died.

So yes, I write about sluts and whores because as everyone knows, you tend to write about the things you know. And I do like sluts and whores, just not the ones that lie to me and cheat on me.

So be forewarned - if you click on a Just Plain Bob story you will be getting sluts, whores and husbands who do not kill, maim and destroy. There are other things you will rarely find in a Just Plain Bob story. Even though I try to mirror real life my stories all take place in StoryLand. In StoryLand STDs and unwanted pregnancies do not exist unless the author feels like they may add something to the story. Bad things do not happen in StoryLand unless the author so wills it and no amount of "You should have..." in comments and feedback will change a story already posted.

Lastly, I will touch on a truth. None of what I have written here means shit because the same readers will still read the same stories that they profess to hate and make the same comments they have always made. Knowing this, I will deliberately post stories that will have them frothing at the mouth.

It is the least I can do for an adoring public.

Thank you!

Just Plain Bob
justplainbob@awesomeauthors.org